Tails of War...

Calliope

The Tale of a Police Horse During the Blitz

Story by *Diane Condon-Boutier*
Illustrations by *Elisabeth Gontier*

Other titles in the series Tails of War:
Spooky: the Adventures of a Ship's Cat in WWII
Zip: the Story of a Carrier Pigeon in WWII

Other works by Diane Condon-Boutier:
Through These Doors; the Manoir at Bout l'Abbé
(a historical fiction novel for adults)

Calliope: The Tale of a Police Horse in WWII

For a favorite policeman, Terry, who didn't ride a horse but who spent a career looking after the public and in particular teaching children about the dangers of the modern world through the words of a dog named McGruff

My name is Calliope. I am a horse, but not just any horse. I am a horse attached to the London Metropolitan Police Services and I am beautiful. People tell me so every day.

The groom who brushes my coat - keeping it glossy and clean - tells me.

The young man who keeps my fittings and saddle polished and shiny, tells me. My handler Edward, who trims and braids my mane before taking me out to work, tells me what a fine mare I am.

The smith who comes to change my shoes tells me. And the people who line the streets when I parade by cheer and flatter me with enthusiastic "ooh's!" and "ah's!". So, I know that I am beautiful.

I've also been given an unusual name. I couldn't be called Sally or Bess like ordinary horses. My name comes from Greek mythology. Calliope was the goddess of poetry and eloquence. She was a muse, a daughter of Zeus. So, by telling this story I'll have to do my best to tell it well, making certain to live up to my namesake.

I lead an extraordinary life. I live in a warm, brickwork stable in central London. It is clean and pleasant. I eat well. And sometimes I'm taken out into the countryside on holiday, to enjoy fresh air, thick green grass and sunshine.

Edward is particularly kind to me and we know each other well. We've been working together for several years now.

Our work days revolve around patrolling the busy streets of London, keeping an eye on the activities of the Londoners.

Sometimes Edward and I have to chase down a pick-pocket to arrest them. We assist the Bobbies patrolling on foot. They alert us to an incident and we help pursue the culprit. Once a trouble-maker sees me dashing towards him, he pretty much stops, knowing I can easily out-run him. I am fast and impressive, as well as beautiful.

Not every horse can become a police horse. I was chosen for my strength and height. I am 15 hands tall and have been trained not to be frightened by loud noises. I have heard gun shots, motor vehicle horns and engine backfires. Crowds don't bother me, nor does shouting. I know Edward's voice and understand his commands. He doesn't need to shout at me, instead he uses his knees to press his wishes into my sides. I know which direction he expects me to go and how fast he wants me to get there, just by feeling the pressure from his thighs and knees. I can stop immediately when I feel him lift his weight from the saddle if he's about to jump off. We are a perfectly matched team, Edward and me.

Lately, I've noticed the arrival of many soldiers in London. Edward and our fellow policemen have been talking about war. You see, the year is 1940 and England has been in conflict with Nazi Germany for about nine months now.

This is the second time that England has been at war with Germany this century and many of our policemen tell stories about what

happened in London during the Great War which lasted from 1914 through 1918. Many of them had to go off to fight the Germans. They have very bitter memories of battlefields in continental Europe: in France and in Belgium.

I hear them discussing places with unusual names like Ypres, the Somme, Vimy, Passchendaele and Verdun. They shake their heads sadly and clap each other on the back when those places are mentioned.

They remember the terrible conditions in the trenches where rats lived amongst the soldiers and a terrible sickness called the Spanish Flu killed almost as many men as did the bullets of enemy soldiers.

They also tell of terrible floating balloons called zeppelins which flew slowly across the London sky, dropping bombs onto the city streets. This struck fear into the hearts of Londoners, causing extensive damage not only to morale but to buildings and homes in the city center.

I find that sort of thing particularly cowardly. Soldiers are at war with one another and should keep their fighting to battlefields, far away from cities. Ordinary people - women and children - should not be in danger of bombs falling from the skies, killing them in their beds!

So far in this war, we haven't seen a zeppelin, although London city officials have prepared fallout shelters in case they show up once again. I hope that this war will be nothing like the last, because even if I can run down a criminal, I cannot fly and wouldn't be helpful in arresting airplanes or zeppelins.

****

This morning, like so many other mornings, Edward and I exit the station house to go out on patrol. It's quite early and people are leaving their homes to go to work, walking briskly toward the tube stations leading into the underground transportation system crisscrossing the city beneath us.

The headmaster at the corner school has opened the gate to the play yard and children are streaming toward the school from every direction. I love this part of the day.

I can tell they enjoy greeting us as they start their day.

"Calliope! How's a good girl today?" A young boy approaches and I reach out to sniff his hand.

Edward allows them to pat my neck and stroke my velvet nose.

I blow at them in greeting and toss my perfectly trimmed mane, feeling pleased at the attention.

"How are you today, Billy?" asks Edward. "Any letters from your father?"

Billy rubs my white blaze and I pull a bit on the reins to reach toward his hand, seeking more attention. "Yes sir, we heard from him just yesterday."

"Everything going well, I hope?"

"My Mum misses him so much, that I almost wish he wouldn't write us. She cries all night after getting his letters."

"Aw, your poor mother. She wants this war to be over, just like the rest of us. You keep working hard at school and don't give her any extra trouble, you hear?"

"Yes sir, I will do! Bye Callie! Be a good horse!" Billy gives my nose one last rub before dashing off through the gate.

An attractive young woman dressed in a pretty flowered dress catches my attention as she approaches the gate, walking hand in hand with a small, curly-haired girl. My eyes are drawn to the child's bright red shoes. I've never seen anything quite like them.

"Look mama! A zebra!"

Edward laughs and the young mother swings the little girl up into her arms, a bit shy and wary of Edward and me.

I snort and shake my mane. A zebra? Hardly so! I look nothing like a zebra!

The mother takes a step backwards. "No, ma chérie, that's a horse. Zebras only live in Africa." The mother has a lovely singsong accent when she speaks.

"They do not. We saw one at the zoo last summer with Papa."

Edward pipes up, while urging me closer to the mother and child. "I shouldn't think Calliope likes being called a Zebra, dearie. She's a fine horse, tall and strong. Zebras are small, and they have stripes all over their bodies. You don't see any stripes on Calliope, now do you?"

"No, but it rains so much here, they could have all washed away!"

"Well, for that you're right! We get our fair share of rain! And where do you come from? Somewhere with more sunshine, I'm guessing?"

"My husband is English, but Antoinette was born in Toulouse, in the south of France. That's where I am from," explains the young mother.

"Ah! The south of France! The land of cheese and frogs' legs!" laughs Edward. "We leave the legs on our froggies here, Miss Antoinette, so if I find any missing their legs we'll know who's guilty, won't we?"

"Oh, we wouldn't eat your English frogs, Sir! It's a special kind of French frog, from warm ponds in the south. That's what makes them so tasty. They live near where the garlic grows!" Antoinette retorts.

"Just so, just so, little one. Say, those are some snappy red slippers you're wearing there, dearie!"

"They are new shoes Maman bought for me before leaving France. She said we'll want to bring as many pretty things with us as possible since London children always dress in brown or navy blue. I think brown clothing is perfectly hideous, don't you?"

Edward lifts his head and laughs before speaking to the girl's mother. "She's a perky little thing, isn't she? Well, let me welcome you both to the land of fish and chips. Calliope and I hope you get on well here! If you need anything just ask us, and we'll be glad to help you out. Now off to school with you, young Miss, before the head master comes out to scold you and your red shoes for being late!"

Antoinette's mother bends to speak closely to her daughter, smooths the child's dress and runs a hand over her wild curls.

"Alright my love, it's time for you to go into class now. Remember to be polite and listen closely to what the teacher says. Try not to talk too much. Teachers like children to listen, not to talk. I'll be here at the gate when school is over."

"Alright, Maman! Don't you worry, I'll be fine!" Antoinette waves goodbye before standing up straight, taking a deep breath and marching off into the schoolyard: a small soldier setting off to face the enemy.

Edward leans over my neck, laying his elbows across the front of the saddle. "First day in the trenches, is it?" he enquires of the mother, who watches Antoinette bravely winding through crowds of shouting children.

She turns back to speak with him. "Yes, and I've got to get off to work. I'm starting a new job as a translator for the government. I wish I too had new, red shoes to give me courage on my first day!"

As she turns away, she remembers her manners and stops to reach a hand out for Edward to shake. "I'm sorry, I forget to introduce myself. My name is Roseline Dunfield."

"Ah! I knew there was a pretty name to go along with such a lovely accent! Welcome to London, Roseline Dunfield. I am Officer Edward Watson, at your service, mum. I can't give you new shoes, Mrs. Dunfield, but I can say that you'll do just fine at your first day of work. And little Antoinette will be fine as well. Calliope and I will keep an eye out for her, don't you worry yourself!"

"You're very kind Officer Watson. And thank you for your offer!" As she steps away, she gives me a gentle pat on the nose and whispers, "You certainly don't look like a zebra, Calliope. You're a fine horse indeed and don't let anyone tell you different!"

I puff my thanks at her compliment, making her dark curls dance, then watch her hurry off to be swallowed into the crowd rushing down the steps to the tube station opposite the school.

Once the children are settled in class and the headmaster shuts the gate to the yard, we set off on our usual rounds of the neighborhood.

Like most days, we stop to speak with Mr. Wilson as he sweeps invisible dust from the front step of his butcher shop. We salute Mike, the young newspaper hawker, with his bag of newsprint slung across one shoulder. Mr. Perkins looks up from the workbench in the cobbler shop to wave at us as we pass by, moving upstream in the traffic of motorcars and buses carrying busy Londoners around their fast-paced lives in spite of the threat of enemy bombing. It is an ordinary day.

Near the end of the working day, our last stop before making our way to the station house for our supper is the corner school. Shouting children swarm out to be gathered by waiting parents. Some set off hand in hand - brothers and sisters, or next-door neighbors - back to their homes and waiting teacups with mashed turnip and potato pie meals. We are here to make certain everyone is taken care of.

Little, red-shoed Antoinette is waiting, standing on tiptoe looking for a familiar flowered dress. None appears. The other children skip off and leave her waiting alone by the gate.

Edward and I approach the corner. "Young miss? Your mother must be held up at work. Calliope and I will wait with you for a bit, if you don't mind?"

"She said I should wait here, but I know my way home. We're living with Daddy's Great-Aunt Imelda, just off Southwark street. I'll wait for a few more minutes but if she doesn't come, I can walk there myself. I remember the way."

"Well, miss, I think we should wait just a bit longer, don't you think?"

Edward and Antoinette begin to chat about her first day of school and all that she learned, about her lessons and what homework was expected of her. A half hour passes quickly and the headmaster comes down the front steps, locks the door and crosses the schoolyard.

"Well, wouldn't you guess that the French wouldn't be on time!" he grumbles. Turning to Antoinette he adds, "Your mother has a watch? Doesn't she know what time school finishes? Where are you to go? Do you know where you live?" Without waiting for answers to these questions, he continues grumbling to Edward and me. "I can't understand how these foreigners can be so careless with their offspring! Drop them off and never come back.

Negligent people, the French are! And us, always bailing them out of trouble!"

Antoinette opens her mouth to snap at these insults, her cheeks flushed almost as red as her shoes. I can see her remembering her mother's advice - thinking before speaking – as she bites her lips to make sure they stay closed.

"Mister Headmaster! With all due respect sir, this child is waiting for her mother and might already be a bit worried. Let's not make it worse than it already is. I'll wait with her until her mother comes if you need to leave straight away, sir."

"Alright, but only if you're sure, Officer. I do have a church meeting tonight and I need my tea before I go. I cannot wait about for hours on end for somebody to show up and claim this child!" spouts the Headmaster. He turns and bustles off down the sidewalk, mumbling to himself as he crosses the street "…red shoes, indeed! What is the world coming to?"

"Well, he's a busy man, now isn't he? Don't you worry yourself about his words, young miss. He's just in a hurry, is all."

"He's an unpleasant person, Officer. I don't like him very much at all. What do you think?"

"Now, now, we must be kind when speaking of our elders! Let's see about getting you home. Do you want a ride on Calliope?"

I shake my mane in agreement. I am quite strong enough to carry this child on my back. I rather like her red shoes, they shine like poppies through the failing light of the afternoon.

Edward dismounts and lifts her into the saddle. Taking my reins, he leads me off at a walk towards a street near Southwark and Great-Aunt Imelda's flat, Antoinette chattering and giggling the entire way.

****

The next morning Edward and I are near the corner school as usual.

"Morning, Billy! And hello, young Susan! You're looking perky today!" Edward greets some of the children as they come and pet my nose just before entering the gate to the yard. Others are too shy to approach but those who do feel special, because I make them welcome.

A familiar pair of red shoes is skipping down the sidewalk, the owner pulling on Mrs. Roseline Dunfield's hand.

"Hurry Mama! I want to say hello to Calliope! She carried me all the way home yesterday!"

"Good morning Mrs. Dunfield! And how are you today?" Edward nods a greeting from the saddle.

"Officer Watson! I'm so glad to see you here this morning! I don't know how to thank you for bringing Antoinette home yesterday. I got caught up working on a rather large dossier and couldn't get away. My husband's Great-Aunt said you rode my daughter right up to the front door!"

Edward lifted his hand to ward off the flow of thanks. "It's nothing, Mum, I'll do it again, anytime you need us. I promised I'd look out for Antoinette and I will. Just like all the other children. It's my job, you see? We all have jobs to do and yours is important, I'm sure. Translating important documents for the government, secret messages to the French, I'll bet!"

Roseline's face takes on a serious look. "I do apologize but I'm really not allowed to speak of my work. I hope you understand. But, I hope I won't put you to any inconvenience again, Officer Watson. Thank you once more, for doing me such a favor yesterday!"

"Understand completely, Mum. Secret stuff. Important work."

Antoinette smiles up at me and I bend my head down to her level, so she might stroke the white blaze on my nose. "I've brought you some carrot peels, Calliope! To thank you for the ride home yesterday!"

I gently take the end of one of the orange strips of vegetable from her fingertips and give a tug. The handful of peelings falls to the sidewalk.

Edward dismounts as Antoinette scrambles to gather them up again. "Lay them flat on your open palm for her. Calliope needs to see what you've got, look at the size, so as to grab only the peels and not your fingers. She's very careful if you hold your hand flat open, like this." Edward places one strip of peel across his palm, holds it up to me and I lick it off his hand with my lips. "Now you try."

I lower my head and stretch my nose out to her tiny hand, piled high with carrot peels. She giggles as I snuffle them off her hand.

"That tickles! She's got little hairs all over her lips!" Antoinette is delighted.

So am I. I love carrots, peels and all. I munch happily then look for more, snuffling the child's hand, arm and hair, searching for any other scraps. Her curls blow backwards into her face.

The headmaster steps out to ring the bell.

"You hurry along, miss! Calliope and I will be here when you get out of school." Edward waves as the red shoes scamper across the cobblestone yard.

"I'm off too, before I show up late! Thank you again, Officer Watson!" Mrs. Dunfield smiles and waves.

Edward returns the wave, watching the flowered dress hurry across the crossroads to the underground entrance.

I can see that a pattern might be starting here, a new task to add to our ritual of stops. We'll be keeping an eye on Antoinette and her red shoes.

****

Days turn to weeks and I've carried Antoinette back to her Great Aunt's flat more times than I can count. The situation in London is becoming more and more worrisome. Enemy airplanes have begun streaking across the sky at all hours of the day and night. Buildings have been targeted by their bombs, causing great fires to break out.

Air-raid sirens regularly peal out a shrieking call, urging Londoners to race to the tube stations and cellars which have been equipped as fallout shelters. As soon as night falls, heavy curtains are drawn across the windows of the city, street lamps stay unlit, and people mostly stay indoors so that the German airplanes can't find the lights of London from the sky.

Edward and I help keep crowds of people calm, urging them to walk quickly, but not to push one another or to panic. Because when people run around and begin pushing one another, someone is going to accidentally get hurt. We make sure that order is kept when raids take place during our tour of duty. We've not had any bombs fall in our neighborhood. Not yet, anyway.

The numbers of children still attending school has dropped. Many have been evacuated to their own great aunts or grandparents living far away from the city and the threat of enemy bombing. Edward and I have been more careful of the safety of the children coming and going from our corner school.

One morning, it's Great Aunt Imelda who accompanies a sad faced Antoinette to school.

"And just what has taken your smile away this morning, young lady?" asks Edward.

"Maman is gone," mumbles Antoinette through a stubbornly unhappy bottom lip.

"And where has she gone off to?" asks Edward.

"She wouldn't say! And we don't have secrets from one another! Maman says it's not nice to keep secrets from people you love! But now it's her that's got one and she's keeping it from me!" A little red shoe stamps the pavement in anger.

I can't help reaching down and blowing into Antoinette's curls which obligingly lift and fly into her face. She giggles just as Great Aunt Imelda places a stern hand on Antoinette's shoulder.

"Now that's quite enough, young lady. No theatrics from children, do you hear? Your mother is working. End of story." The old lady turns to Edward. "Do forgive that outburst, Officer. And you too, lovely horse!" She pats my nose and I snort a response.

Edward stops the old lady with a question just as she turns to leave. "And won't you and Antoinette be leaving

the city to a safer spot outside of town, Mum? Many people have already left, you know."

"Yes, well, I've lived through the bombing and hardship of one war without running away, so I guess I can do it once again, can't I?"

"But surely, for the child, Mum?" Edward insists.

"Can't protect children from life too long, now can we? And who would be there to let her mother in when she gets back? Now, good day to you, Officer and horse!" Great Aunt Imelda totters down the sidewalk using her cane.

Antoinette waits until her Aunt has gone around the corner before saying "She's not a very, VERY nice lady, is she?"

"Alright, young lady, into school you go! You've got your teacher waiting for you!" When Antoinette gets out of earshot, he leans down to whisper in my ear. "No, she's not a very, VERY nice lady. But it's not kind of us to judge our elders, is it, Calliope?"

I bob my head in agreement and snort out the smell of moth balls left behind in my nostrils from Great Aunt Imelda's gloves. No indeed, not very, VERY.

****

Days pass and Great Aunt Imelda walks Antoinette to school and Edward and I carry her home in the afternoon with no sign of her mother's pretty flowered dress. Antoinette wilts a bit with every passing day.

I do my best to cheer her up. I snuffle her ears, blow into her curls, toss my mane when she's on my back and skip a step or two just to listen to her squeal with delight. Our happy moments last from the school yard to the street just off Southwark.

Nights are punctuated with screaming air raid sirens warning of bombs dropping from the sky. The first raids result in entire streets exploding and whole buildings reduced to piles of collapsed walls, doors and windows. Each morning people pick through the mess looking for their belongings. Neighbors take in neighbors who have lost everything, squeezing extra families into already cramped quarters, sharing what's left.

Edward and I spend longer hours on the streets, assisting people in need, trying to answer the questions of those who have lost everything. Londoners struggle to piece together their lives every morning as if nothing horrible had happened the night before. But I can see the effect the war is having on their spirits.

They don't pat my nose anymore. Few stop to talk to me or to tell me I'm beautiful. Edward has stopped braiding my mane in the morning. And there are never any cheers when we pass by on the street. It's true that Mr. Wilson nods a greeting from his front step and that Mike waves a newspaper at us, but the headlines he's shouting are more and more frightening. It sounds as though the enemy troops are winning the war.

"France falls!" he shouts one morning and the passersby cringe as Mike spreads awful news into the grey London air.

"This is a sad day, Calliope," says Edward. "The enemy is getting closer and closer."

When we stop at the corner school, Edward calls out a greeting to Billy who is dragging his feet through the running water of the gutter.

"You'll wreck your shoes doing that Billy! Step up onto the pavement before your mum gets after you!"

"She won't even notice, Officer. She's been in her bedroom and hasn't come out for two days."

"Oh my," Edward guesses there's been bad news from Billy's father. "Well, all the more reason to keep from harming your things, then." Edward's knees urge me closer to Billy. I stretch my nose and knock off his cap, hoping to bring the boy out of his sad mood.

Billy throws his arms around my neck, burying his face as he bursts into tears. I lay my ears back in surprise just as Edward swings his weight to the ground.

"Here now, lad! What's the matter?" Edward bends to lay a hand on Billy's shoulder. Billy's not letting go of my neck, but that's fine. I take a step closer, making it easier for him to cling to me.

A muffled voice spits out a word here and there. "...prisoner ...Dunkirk...not coming home!"

"Oh my!" repeats Edward. "Well, it's bad news, that is! But there is the one thing to remember, Billy...that your brave dad's done his duty for his country and is a prisoner. That means when the war is over, he'll be coming back home to you and your mum."

Billy shoulders shake and he wraps his fingers in my mane as Edward tries to find the right words of comfort. "...and there's some that can't say that much, Billy. It could be different. It might have been a lot worse. Now you remember that, lad, and take heart. He'll be coming home one of these days, your dad will. You just wait and see."

I reach down Billy's back and gave a tug on his jacket with my teeth, hoping to break the spell of sadness hovering about us. Edward bends to the ground and picks up Billy's cap, slapping the dust off.

"Now, while you're waiting for that to happen, the school master's waiting to teach you all the things you need to know to grow up and make your dad proud. So, if I were you, I'd get in there and get to work learning everything I could, so I was ready when he comes back."

Great Aunt Imelda and Antoinette show up just then. The little girl notices Billy rubbing away streaks of tears and runs to grab his hand.

"Oh Billy! Are you sad? Whatever it is will be fine, I'm sure of it! Could you help me with my poem recitation? I need to practice before Headmaster drills me! May I say it to you first?"

The two of them walk through the gate, one chattering and the other quiet, but listening.

"Well that was kind of her, don't you say, mum?"

"Yes, she's a strange child," replies Great Aunt Imelda before turning on her cane. "Good day to you, Officer and horse!"

I snort a reply as Officer Watson tips his hat to her back. "Antoinette's got a point, not very, VERY." I can't help but toss my head in agreement.

That night as I'm standing on three hooves, dozing peacefully in my stall, the sirens go off once again. I hear the groom running down the brick hallway, throwing open the gates to the horse stalls.

My saddle is flung onto my back and he's quickly reaching beneath my belly, hooking the buckles.

Edward rushes in and checks my halter, then turns back to grab a length of rope before leading me out into the hall. The other horses are being led out as well and it's a great commotion of clattering hooves on the brickwork.

Out on the street, people are hurrying through their front doors, clinging to children and carrying their pets with them on their way to their prescribed fallout shelters.

Edward swings into the saddle just as an elderly woman passes carrying a bird cage with two canaries squeaking in the panic of being woken and jostled about. Another passerby is struggling with a wicker hamper producing the frantic meows of an unhappy cat.

All around us people are moving along the dark street at different speeds, bumping into and tripping over each other. Children are crying and parents are scolding, while everyone tries to move as quickly as possible.

Someone crashes into my backside and I let out a surprised squeal and snort. My hooves clatter on the street cobbles and I can feel the atmosphere of growing fear through pounding hearts and strained breathing.

"Easy now, girl. We've got to help get these people safely underground. Stay quiet!" Edward urges me into the street to help direct the pedestrians.

From atop my back his vantage point gives him a better view and his voice carries over the crowds of running people.

"This way, another hundred yards down the north pavement to the tube entrance! No pushing. Stay calm! Keep moving!"

Over and over, he shouts the same words to people rushing down the street. "That's right keep moving this way! The entrance is just ahead! Keep moving, no pushing! Remain calm!"

Suddenly, from far overhead the noise of a droning engine is heard.

A woman shrieks in panic, "God save us! It's them! The bombers are coming this way!"

As the noise grows progressively louder I begin to shift uneasily.

Edward hold my reins tight, and bends to speak in my ear. "No moving, girl. Stay steady." Then he sits upright and continues speaking to the people hurrying through the darkness. "Don't panic, just keep moving, you'll get there faster if you just keep moving steadily, No pushing!"

In the night sky a swarm of airplanes approach and the noise is steadily increasing. I can't hear Edward any longer as more men begin shouting and more women are screaming.

The planes appear to be moving very slowly and it seems to take a very long time for the first bombs to fall all the way out of the sky onto the pavement at the end of the street.

As the first bomb hits the ground, the pavement shudders under my hooves and I repress an instinctive urge to bolt. I can't help rearing my front hooves off the ground but Edward holds tight and I remember my training.

Me tearing off down the street in the dark is not going to help anything at all. I too, must stay calm. I blow hard and toss my head as a German plane passes just above us. The noise is unbearable. I flatten my ears as Edward ducks low over my neck.

There's a reverberation, then a shock, a gaseous smell and finally a wave of heat before chunks of brickwork, wood and glass fly in every direction at the same time. My body is pelted with flying debris of every imaginable kind. The noise is deafening. Edward is knocked to the ground, still holding my reins.

I am overcome with a thoughtless urge to run, fast.

The pavement ahead of me breaks under the impact of another bomb landing just ahead of us. Edward holds tight and shouts to me as I stumble sideways and fall.

My ears are filled with panicked shrieking and I realize some of it is me making a lot of noise. My hooves flail as I try to regain my feet. First, I struggle to my knees and a sharp pain shoots through my foreleg. I fall back to my side.

I look down and see blood. My blood. I've never seen my own blood before. I can smell it, too. A metallic tang, both familiar and unfamiliar at the same time. My nostrils flare wide open both to breathe in the smell and then to expel it as quickly as possible. I don't like it.

Edward is on his knees at my side, one hand on my halter, speaking calming words as he runs the other hand down my legs, each in turn. He's feeling for breaks to the long bones. Broken legs are fatal for horses. I trust him and I am afraid to stand until he finishes.

Edward finds the bleeding spot on my leg and removes a long shard of glass with a gentle but firm tug. He presses the skin around the spot and listens for me to squeal in pain. But while it's painful, it hurts much less now that the glass is removed. Edward ties his handkerchief around my leg in a makeshift bandage, then stands.

One pat on the neck urging me to roll onto my knees, then up onto all fours. I'm quivering with shock but Edward's hands run all over my body, testing me for other wounds. I can feel many spots pinch in minor pain as he passes over them and his hands pick up more blood as they reveal numerous nicks and cuts but nothing serious. Yet, his touch reassures and calms me. As we stand getting

our wits about us for a short instant, another pair of German planes rumble through the sky just above our street. As they pass overhead in agonizing slowness, every face in the city turns skyward to watch, estimating where the bombs will land as the bellies of the planes open and dark, heavy shapes begin their fall.

The shouts and cries of those a few blocks father along reach us after the reverberation of their bombs calms. They are living the hell we've just survived- each city block in its turn, like the progression of a parade of falling dominoes.

The initial shock of the bombing fades and we slowly come to our senses. Edward mounts and we turn to our task at hand, leaving the others farther along the street to do the same. People are climbing to their feet, brushing themselves off, turning and searching the immediate surroundings for their companions. Names are called out, and answers are shouted.

"Nancy! Nancy! Where are you?"

"I'm here!"

"Tommy!"

"Ma! I'm here! I'm fine!"

In the light of burning buildings, I see a cane and a wool tweed hat lying on the pavement. They look familiar. I lead Edward toward them and bend to sniff the hat. Moth balls.

Then I notice a single red slipper. Half covered in dust, it sits among the rubble as if wounded, the small strap unbuckled.

Dread fills my heart and I whinny and fling my head, pulling against the bit. Edward finally notices the shoe.

"Oh no! Antoinette!" He whispers. Swinging off the saddle, he bends to gently touch the little shoe, shouting this time. "Antoinette! Imelda! Antoinette!" Then quietly he whispers a prayer, "Please, please! Don't let her be hurt!"

Edward scans the street to the left and right, hoping to see them: the owners of the red shoe and cane. Nothing and everything.

People carrying out their own searches, identical to ours, are turning over pieces of furniture, lifting doors from stairways, removing stones obstructing door frames, all the while calling out names, over and over as their voices become hoarse with churning dust.

Edward continues to shout out "Antoinette!" and drops the shoe as he lifts and pushes and uncovers the small opening to a stairwell leading to an underground cellar.

"Callie! Here girl!" Edward grabs the rope and wraps it around an oak beam jammed across the stairwell. He slips the other end under the leather straps passing beneath my belly securing my saddle. "Pull, Callie!" Shouting to me, he scrambles back into the saddle and presses his knees into my sides turning me away from the sidewalk. My reins are taut and I take a cautious step feeling the rope pull on the saddle. Edward turns in the saddle looking over his shoulder to judge the progress. Nothing.

"Pull, Callie! Harder! You can do it! Pull!" The beam squeaks across the stone foundations, moving just a few inches before jamming once again. I puff and snort with the effort. My muscles are trembling.

Edward jumps back off the saddle and bends into the space leading down to the cellar. "I hear something! Pull Callie!" This time with no weight in the saddle to hold it on, the taut rope begins to shift the saddle on my back, inching its way out of place, sliding along my back.

I feel someone else hoist onto my back and am surprised to see a trail of flowered material brush by my face. A softer voice bends toward my ear. "Please Callie, pull hard! For me!"

My job isn't over, I push with the heavy muscles in my haunches, straining forward as I pull with all the weight of my body, step by tiny step, my hooves slipping on the cobbles. I can feel drops of blood ooze through the wound on my leg and dozens of tiny sore spots all telling me to stop because this work hurts.

The beam groans in resistance, refusing to budge. But, I'm not giving up. I'm pulling for Edward, for Great Aunt Imelda, for tiny, red-shoed Antoinette and for the woman with the top-secret job perched on my back urging me to give it my all.

I take a deep breath, filling my chest with enough air to send a jolt of energy to my aching muscles. It's with the biggest heave I can manage that the beam finally pulls free with a clatter and thump.

My rider jumps down as Edward carefully climbs down
into the stairwell. Mrs. Roseline Dunfield follows.

As they disappear from my sight, I am overwhelmed with
curiosity and turn to stand at the edge of the hole, pawing
the ground, whinnying and generally showing my
impatience. From inside, I hear muffled voices and crying.
I reach down and sniff at the wounded red shoe, plucking
the loose strap from the pavement with my teeth.

Finally, a mass of curly hair pokes up through the rubble.

I toss my head in greeting. The red slipper flings around
my nose dangling by its strap, waving in greeting to its

owner. One by one, three more heads emerge. Great Aunt Imelda is helped though the jagged opening, until each one of my friends is safe on the sidewalk. There is much hugging and patting and joyous greetings exchanged while I whinny and whicker and stamp my hooves with relief, the shoe dancing in my teeth. They turn to me, disheveled and filthy with dirt and ash. Antoinette gives a shout of pure happiness as the others laugh.

"Callie! You've found my shoe!" Antoinette reaches to retrieve it from my teeth, slips it on and buckles the strap.

I cannot resist bending over her and blowing in her hair to make her curls dance. Her face is streaked with dust and tears. Antoinette giggles.

"I'm afraid I need a bath, and so do you, Callie!" A puff of dust rises as she strokes the dirt from my once white blaze.

In spite of all the dirt and all the scrapes and cuts, I have never felt more beautiful.

THE END

Tails of War

The "Tails of War" series is based on the recipients of the Dickin Medal of Honor, awarded up to this day, to the animals who assist troops in wartime. While the series is fiction, it is historical fiction, meaning that I've chosen to take the stories of the flesh and blood recipients of the Dickin Medal and mesh them together to create a piece of fiction designed to incite the curiosity of young minds.

History doesn't often find a spot at the top of the 'adored school subjects' list. I believe that storytelling is one way to change that. Stories can lead students to history. This is the purpose of "Tails of War".

To that end, I highly encourage parents, teachers and young people who have questions about the background of Calliope, of Edward and more particularly about Roseline and Antoinette, to do a little digging.

The horses who were awarded the Dickin Medal were brave animals who came to the aid of an entire city of victims during Nazi Germany's Blitzkrieg of London. They stayed calm. They did not bolt. Instead, they directed a panic-stricken population to the relative safety of fallout shelters through the dark of night, through the terror of bombing, and at great cost to their own safety. They were, of course, mounted by policemen, who were most courageous: the 'Officer Edwards' of the London Metropolitan Police. Without their guidance, the casualty rate amongst the civilian population would have, without a doubt, been much greater.

The character of Roseline is loosely based on one of the most famous female figures of WW2: Violette Szabo. Elisabeth Gontier's illustrations of Roseline reflect that.

Violette was an attractive, young Franco-British woman who chose to become involved in the British Special Operations Executive or S.O.E. Her husband, Etienne, fought for France. She became a spy. Their daughter, Tania, who was of course much younger than our Antoinette, was left behind in England, in the care of childminders during Violette's two expeditions into Nazi occupied France. Neither of Tania's parents survived the war. They are thought to be the most decorated married couple of WW2.

Please look up their story. Please, look at the profiles of the other 54 women of the S.O.E. Look at the stories of the recipients of the Dickin Medal: the 4 horses, 32 pigeons, 28 dogs and a cat who gave their courage and loyalty to their human friends, sometimes at the cost of their own lives.

But, before I leave you to your research, I must give my most profound thanks to those eagle-eyed friends who hunt down typos - and grammatical mistakes in the French and English versions, and to those who respond to my emails begging for tidbits of information such as the color of the London mounted police uniforms in 1940, etc. Your indulgence and boundless patience is much appreciated.

Last but most important are my most grateful thanks to the countless historians who have come before me, documenting the details which successfully bring to life the sacrifices of those who shaped our world.

Because, if the word 'history' contains the word 'story', there's a very good reason.

Diane Condon-Boutier